MONSTER OF CHRONOS

R G AADHAV

Copyright © R G Aadhav 2024
All Rights Reserved.

ISBN

Paperback: 979-8-89588-902-2
Hardcase: 979-8-89632-742-4

This book has been published with all efforts taken to make the material error-free after the consent of the author. However, the author and the publisher do not assume and hereby disclaim any liability to any party for any loss, damage, or disruption caused by errors or omissions, whether such errors or omissions result from negligence, accident, or any other cause.

While every effort has been made to avoid any mistake or omission, this publication is being sold on the condition and understanding that neither the author nor the publishers or printers would be liable in any manner to any person by reason of any mistake or omission in this publication or for any action taken or omitted to be taken or advice rendered or accepted on the basis of this work. For any defect in printing or binding the publishers will be liable only to replace the defective copy by another copy of this work then available.

Acknowledgment

I thank the almighty for the blessings. I give my utmost Gratitude to my parents, R. Ganesh and R. Shalini. They encouraged me to read books, attend book fairs, visit all book stores and set me on the path. I also express my special thanks to my grandfather, S. Raju, who inculcated the interest of books in me and praised me constantly to aim high. I do show my gratitude for my Grandmother, G. Malathy, for her support and contribution in my growth. I show my Gratitude to all my teachers, friends, well-wishers and relatives. Their words helped me and their unwavering support contributed to the making of this book. I also thank both my schools, Velammal Vidhyashram, Surapet-Chennai and Maharishi Vidya Mandir, Mogappair-Chennai for their educational support and encouragement. Once again, I thank everyone.

$\mathcal{P}$ROLOGUE

EGYPT

3 88 B.C., Doom first came. The Egyptians were doing their daily routine. Most Egyptians were scribes, artisans, and field workers. However, the Egyptians in this scenario were not the slaves of Pharaoh. This band had just escaped from their cruel Pharaoh, longing for freedom. But fate had other plans. It would give them a future far worse than being Pharaoh's slave. They didn't expect that this day would change their lives or, more likely, end their lives. They were alarmed that the Pharaoh's soldiers were on their search. The Pharaoh was hell-bent on capturing them and making an example of them. But now they threw aside their thoughts and focused on their current state. They were living joyfully in freedom when the fateful event took place. Out of the blue, a fireball roared from the sky. Screaming as a veil of fear was placed upon their minds. Out of pure terror, they started shouting, "Long live, sun God!" The fireball hit a place, which was not far from the place the Egyptians are

staying. Confusion spread among the Egyptians. A man pushed the baskets violently as he ran. The food fell down just like the Egyptians who are going to fall. They rushed to see a large smoking crater, marking where the fireball had fallen. The scorched ground hummed. Suddenly, the ground started shaking violently. The sand started vibrating. The Egyptians fell upon each other. Huts started breaking. Pots broke. An object never seen before rose from the pit where the fireball had fallen. The object floated in the air, and the Egyptians looked up in awe. Was it Apep (creature of chaos)? It was spherical in shape, and it had an outer covering of an unknown metal. Suddenly, to their shock and absolute terror, tentacles materialized on the object. Hearts pounded, and breathing turned heavy for them. The Egyptians bowed before it in fear of its wrath. However, the sphere needed no absolute terror from them. It only needed their blood.

ATLANTIS

371 BC. They never knew that one day their lives would become a myth. They never knew that their kingdom would sink into the darkest depths. Atlantis was a mighty kingdom. It had very less economic ties with its neighboring kingdom, not that it had many neighboring kingdoms. The

kingdom consisted of a single island. The island had a volcano that had not erupted for many years. Atlantis was a three-circle formation featuring a giant volcano in the middle. Each circle was connected by a pathway or a canal. Between each circle, there was a moat. It was a structured system designed by the greatest architects of the age. The Atlanteans were doing their routine (mostly fishing) when the volcano started releasing smoke fumes. The fumes worried them but not to a large extent. However, some thought that the volcano was going to erupt and left Atlantis. They would soon be proved correct. But many were stubborn and believed that the volcano would not erupt, so they stayed in Atlantis. Days passed without any incident. To the people's shock, a mysterious object rose from the volcano's opening. The object fired a red beam of intense heat, which triggered the volcano. All hell broke loose. The destruction of the kingdom began. Lava shot up, destroying as much as possible. Massive rocks and lava fell upon them and on houses, burning through everything. Their cries silenced by the intense heat. The royal palace was completely eradicated. The kingdom was located near an ocean. Out of the waters, a dark shape rose for a split second and took a major portion of Atlantis with it. People screamed. The horizon was filled with chaos. Even the creature that triggered the volcano got damaged as lava rocks fell. Its machinery started creaking as the lava seeped inside, drawn to the energy source of it, for the source was an exact opposite of the known universe. When the lava seeped into the energy source of the machine, it exploded with an energy explosion larger than that of an atomic bomb. This sunk the kingdom and the mysteries surrounding it were born…

> *"In a single day and night of misfortune,*
> *The island of Atlantis disappeared*
> *into the depths of the sea."*
>
> *Plato, 360 B.C.*

PART 1

CHAPTER 1

2020, it was a hot day. A white ship sailed across the Atlantic waters. The name "GOLDEN WIND" is emblazoned in gold on the ship. Aboard the ship was an adult aged 21 called Ted. Ted was an archaeologist; he even knows ancient myths ranging from Greek to Egypt.. Ted always wears a neatly pressed and crisp brown shirt. Ted is inseparable from his brown bag. His vacation and job plan was to sail on a ship from Florida to Nigeria, take an airplane from Nigeria to Egypt, and then stay in Egypt for a week, spending time looking at pyramids and tombs. Booking a plane at the Egypt airport, which goes to Florida. He could have simply taken a plane from Florida to Egypt, but he wanted to travel by ship and also spend as much time as he could on vacation. Frequently, he talked with his colleague about his work and chatted on different matters. One day they had a talk about Greek deities. It went something like this:

Ted: Hercules would never have killed the Hydra without Iolaus.

Colleague: You're wrong. Hercules could have poured oil on his sword, set it aflame, and then behead the Hydra.

Ted: But Hercules was not smart enough to think that previously.

Colleague: You're just kidding.

Presently on the second level of the ship, inside a room, he was playing chess online with his friend. Even though Ted lost, he argued that his opponent clearly cheated. This argument continued for several minutes. Finally, Ted receded and became silent. He went back to his room and opened his laptop. He was halfway through his work, when the ship shook unnaturally. He raised his eyebrows. He then ignored it and proceeded with his work. But, the ship started shaking violently. The laptop fell down. Ted lost his balance and fell from the bed, but somehow managed to hold and balance a grip. "What was it?" grunted Ted. "Heck, it sounded like Titanic hitting an iceberg," thought Ted. Even though he tried to cool, there was a chill of nervousness down his spine. Nervous and loud voices were heard on the deck of the ship. "What the hell is going on?" he thought and set off for the deck. The deck was a beautiful place. With wooden boards, you could hear the sound of the crashing waves. However, at this particular time, the floorboards rattled, lurched back and forth. On the deck, people were scurrying everywhere and some were shouting while looking at the waters. Ted found everyone looking in awe at something. But Ted apparently mistook their horrific look for awe. As Ted looked into the ocean, he found what had drawn everyone's attention. Around 2,000 yards away, there was a black object rising fast from the Atlantic Ocean. It did not seem man-made or natural. It seemed like it was otherworldly. It seemed like a sphere. Its surface seemed matte. It seemed alien, distant, ancient, and dangerous. There was a rectangle-shaped light source on it which glowed bright blue. There was a circle on it which looked like a yin yang symbol. The machine was huge, like a football pitch could fit in it.

Such were the words that can be used to describe it. It was creating strong ripples and waves, which shook the "Golden Wind." Ted's mouth fell as they looked in awe at the slowly but surely floating object. "What the hell is this?" panicked Ted. Captain William was the first person to break the tension. Captain William matched his ship well. One can say that the captain is the brain, while the ship is the hands and legs. Captain William is a fine sailor. He wears his crisp captain's uniform; he has a large beard. Presently, Captain William shouted to all the people on the deck to go to the second level of the ship. Everyone, including Ted, went to the second level of the ship; everyone pushed at each other in their rat race to hopeful salvation.

Ted looked at the window in horror. People were fear-struck. Somehow the climate had turned into a dreadful storm. Light clashed and rain fell like rocks. Six tentacles had materialized in the object's front. The object started heading toward the golden wind. People started screaming. Some said this was a sign from the gods and they are making us pay for our insolence and pride. The tentacles started lashing at the ship furiously. The tentacles lashed at the ship in a violent collision, which thrashed the whole ship brutally. The ship coughed and shook. Railing fell on some poor fellow's head. Walls fell on top. Floorboards creaked and broke. Rushing water entered through the punctured ship. People started screaming. There was a commotion on the second level. On the deck, they could hear the feeble voice of Captain William shouting that the ship's hull is damaged and the ship is going to sink. Through the hole in the ceiling, Ted saw Captain William with his hands clenched and bellowing at the sphere.

The people ran toward the deck to take a long boat. Rain splattered on Ted's face. Wind lashed on his face. While running toward the deck, Ted saw three diving suits in an open room. He made a quick decision and snatched one from the holders. As he went to the place where the longboats were located, he saw that the tentacle had destroyed most of the long boats and was snatching screaming people. A longboat flew right over his head. He yelped and ducked, covering his head with his arms and leaving the diving suit to fall on the floor. The boat crashed on the wall behind him and shattered it. He saw that all long boats were already filled and some were about to be filled. But just as a group of people was about to get on a longboat, the tentacle snatched them, and their screaming voices were drowned by the storm. Ted took his diving suit and ran toward the longboat. He threw the diving suit inside the boat and climbed inside it. As he climbed inside the boat, the ship started sinking. Since the longboat was attached to the ship by a rope, it would sink in a few minutes. Ted watched the tentacles break the ship in. By God's grace, there was a knife on the longboat. Ted took it and tried to use it to cut the rope. He tried to cut the rope frantically. As he looked at the sphere, he saw that the yin-yang-like symbol was slowly opening. Inside of it was something that glowed like a reactor of some sort. It was an inverted dome with grids. Just as he cut the ropes connecting to the ship, he saw that the blue rectangular light had turned red. As his boat was moving, he saw that the sphere had risen and was directly above the ship. "No," thought Ted, dreading what is going to happen next. The reactor started glowing, and suddenly it fired a large red beam at the ship. The whole ship exploded. The water rose like a volcano eruption and was barreling toward the longboat. "NO!" screamed Ted just as the full force of the huge mountains of water hit his boat. He lost all consciousness as his brain protected him from the trauma.

"Not every storm of life comes to destroy your ship but set the sail to navigate a new direction to prevent your destruction."

– Selvin Brown

Chapter 2

Ted opened his eyes. The sun was too bright to look at. There is still some pain at the back of his head. He could feel the long boat shaking in the waters of the ocean. Someone said, "Ah, at last you have woken up," said a rough voice. Ted rose upright; there wasn't supposed to be anyone with him. But his eyes were foggy, and all he could see was a blurry figure. "Here," the figure handed him a bottle of water. His throat was parched, so he didn't argue. For the first time in his life, water tasted like nectar. After drinking water, he asked, "Who are you?" Ted's eyesight had returned, and he could see that it was a man in his fifties. He wore a cap, a ruffled white shirt, and black pants. He had a white beard and olive-green eyes. Those olive-green eyes showed his roughness. "Farragut," the man grunted, "captain of that yacht," the man pointed at a white and regular-sized yacht. On it, the word painted was VARUNA.

After 5 days:

Ted was eating some of the food at VARUNA, The yacht. He had not yet lost any hope of returning home. Over the 5 days, he had tried his best to not think about the events in the past few days and about the mysterious object. Ted told Farragut about it, but he thinks Ted is just delusional about the trauma. Ted finished his food. Unsurprisingly, Captain Farragut remained distant and murmured about something. He seemed to avoid Ted. The yacht also seemed to roam aimlessly.

Over the 5 days, Ted learned much about the yacht; it had several recliner sofas all around it. Ted found out that it had a supplies room. Its interior was mostly white, just like its exterior. The floorboards were polished and you wouldn't find a speck of dirt on them. It had 5 bedrooms. He tried to contact anyone, but it was of no use.

At present, Ted was walking down the stairs when he found light coming from a small room, which he had not noticed before. He entered the room and found Farragut sitting on a metal chair. The room was filled with hundreds of maps and instruments. Several books and inscriptions were also present there. "What are you doing?" Ted asked. "Get out," snarled Farragut. "No," said Ted boldly, "You have been avoiding me and murmuring something. What kind of job do you do?" asked

Ted. Farragut completely ignored him. Days like this continued. Ted wasn't able to get a single word from the stubborn man. Ted sighed and let it go. Now, Ted was determined to know the truth. He stopped the man and asked him, "What is your past and what do you do?" Farragut knew that this could no longer continue. Hence, he finally acknowledged Ted.

"If I had known that you would be so curious, I would have left you in that long boat to die of starvation," said Farragut. Ted's face turned red, but he said nothing. Farragut sighed and started explaining, "I was an explorer; my thirst for adventure led me on an expedition to find Atlantis."

At this, Ted's eyes began to glow with excitement. Not noticing it, Farragut continued, "I was born into a wealthy French businessman's family, so money was not a problem. I had two friends, both were younger and greater than me. We searched for Atlantis for around thirty four years, but then in a single night of impending doom I found what I sought for 34 years."

Ted gasped; however, Farragut was sad as if it hurt to tell his story. But he continued, "We found that it is really sunken, so I sent both of them to explore it on a submersible. I could not go because I was sick at that time. And that was the last time

I saw them. I waited for them for days until I bought a new diving vehicle and went inside those accursed waters. As I sank and sank, it didn't get darker like it should in an ocean. I saw ruins of the cursed city and saw the brightest light source I had ever seen in my life at the center of the city. Soon, I found an underwater camera from the submersibles. In order to watch what happened, I left the light source and came back to the yacht. I used my computer and device to see what the camera had recorded. I could see that they were walking toward the light source. Then suddenly something dark huge came, and the camera didn't record any further."

A chill went down Ted's spine. "There are dark things in that accursed city, things which you wouldn't inflict on your worst enemy," said Farragut darkly.

"Enlightenment is scary. Sometimes things look better in the dark."

– David Levithan

CHAPTER 3

The Next Morning:

Triiiing! sounded the alarm. Ted woke up. He brushed his teeth (he had learned that the paste is very sour the hard way) and refreshed himself. He drank a cup of coffee. He remembered his conversation with Farragut the previous day and shivered; the story was still fresh in his mind. He showered and tried to get it out of his mind. However, the story was etched in his mind. Farragut seemed to act differently towards Ted. He talked with him often. Why, Farragut even sought to solve Ted's longing to communicate with others by giving him a satellite phone, one that works anywhere on the phone. Ted was full of excitement as he called his colleague.

"Ted, where the hell are you? Are you injured? I heard that the ship you were traveling on got destroyed," asked his colleague. "I am fine, but how do you know about that thing and what is that?" asked Ted anxiously; he was dreading something. His joy in talking with his friend burned down to ash. "Code Red is the name the military and world governments gave for 'that', and it has entered North America," stammered Ted's friend.

"And one more thing, The Centre for American Archaeology in Kampsville summons you," informed his colleague.

"Why?" asked Ted. But the battery of the satellite phone had run out. Ted looked at Farragut, who just shrugged.

Ted talked about his conversation with his colleague to Farragut, who agreed to drop him at the nearest port to the centre. Ted wished to walk on land again.

A Few Days Later:

The yacht touched a port. Farragut told Ted farewell and gave him a salute. And then he went on his way. Ted hoped that Farragut's mourning heart would heal. Ted got a cab and went on his way to the Centre in Kampsville. On the way, he passed a beautiful house with a lawn. Its price was $80,000, so said a board. Ted sighed as he would never be able to buy that house. He sighed and went on his way.

The Centre for American Archaeology was shaped like a cube. It had four windows on its front and was colored in white and brown. Ted could feel that the building gave off a vibe of oldness.

Its windows were sun screened. It would have been done so to not show the building's interior and artifacts present in it. The entrance, however, seemed quite uninviting to him. It seemed to ask him to go somewhere else, instead of entering it. Ted brushed these thoughts aside and entered. The interior was quite plain. It was white and brown. It didn't have many artifacts either. It seemed too plain and boring and had the vibe of, well, oldness. There weren't any grand decorations or paintings. The wall and the ceiling were quite plain. However, it did have a powerful air conditioner. A single man was waiting for him. He wore a brown jacket and a crinkled pair of jeans. He seemed to be in his sixties. His age might have gotten old but his speaking skills certainly did not. He started briefing. The content of what he spoke was enhanced with his enthusiasm. His posture resembled his unwavering enthusiasm and a hint of his optimism. The man told Ted, "We need you to find this artifact which was mentioned in our inscription; we believe it might hold the key to the solution of this unholy beast. Our inscription says:

"To defeat Chronos, the monster, hunt the weapon of gods which holds the power to unite the heavens and hell. Find it in the land which lost its right on land and was swallowed by an ocean of despair, but remember

what sunk the kingdom was not only a monster, but a being equal to a hundred monsters. So terrifying the true demon is, that the name of it is untold and its true boundaries' bonds are the shackles which chain it to water, unable to set foot on land. Find Hunahpu and conquer DEIMOS.

Now the second lies with the oracle of Apollo, the Cancer shows it. Remember the hero's oath, find the three, older than rocks. Find Xbalanque and conquer Phobos. And then you may conquer war itself."

"Oh," Ted was speechless; his imagination ran wild. "By the way, Cancer here means the constellation," said the man. He also informed Ted that the government has given him lots of funds for this exploration. The man sent Ted on his way with an optimistic smile. Ted thought of the house which he saw on his way to the department and thought of buying it. But he shrugged off his distractions as he knew he had a very important job. On his way back, he saw newspapers swirling with news on the kraken's attack and how the military is going to nuke it. Crowds of people were gathered at churches praying for the help of the almighty. People were scared at this otherworldly threat.

Ted's cab moved past them. He had booked a room at Casinova Rooms and prepared to spend his time there before planning his exploration. Ted waited for some time in the lobby, admiring its beauty and splendid artistic designs of soothing waves, and then opened his room, numbered 108. He kept his belongings there, sat on the cushion, and proceeded to think. He thought of the lines of the poem or, more likely, an inscription:

'To defeat Chronos, the monster, hunt the weapon of gods which holds the power to unite the heavens and hell.'

This line must talk about the code red and the artifact, thought Ted. But he couldn't understand how an artifact could unite hell and heaven.

'Find it in the land that lost its right on land and was swallowed by an ocean of despair.'

Interesting, thought Ted. *What could be such a land?* he wondered. Then the answer slammed into his mind. Then out of the blue, he got the answer: "ATLANTIS." This made him recollect the old captain's words. He shivered and wondered whether this expedition will send him there.

"But remember what sunk the kingdom was not only a monster, but a being equal to a hundred monsters."

"Kingdom," thought Ted, now he was pretty sure the inscription talks about Atlantis. "What else could be a drowned kingdom?" he thought.

But the second part of the line sent a chill down his spine. He knew in the back of his mind that the creature which he encountered in Golden Wind had something to do with the destruction of Atlantis, but there seems to be some eeriness surrounding this specific line. There seems to exist a veil on this line hiding the untold horrors of the city's demise. This line mentions that there exists another one 'demon' which seems to be deadlier than the one which is in America. He brushed aside the thoughts about this line. But his mind wandered to the words of Captain Farragut's story about how his friends met their horrific demise trying to explore the accursed city. Ted brushed aside these thoughts and proceeded to the next line.

'So terrifying is the true demon, that the name of it is untold and its true boundaries are the shackles which chain it to water, unable to set foot on land. Conquer DEIMOS.'

This line again talks about the demon but with a hint that this is an underwater creature which cannot survive on land. This made it clear as water to Ted that there is a connection between this demon and the demise of Captain Farragut's friends. "DEIMOS is the God of Terror, so this means we should control our terror," concluded Ted. Ted by now was so terror-stricken by these lines that he decided to think about the rest later. Anyway, he knew his time was running short and he needed to talk with Farragut soon.

"Work is hard. Distractions are plentiful. And time is short."

– Adam Hochschild

CHAPTER 4

Ted called Captain Farragut in the morning. Fortunately, he was still nearby. Ted told him what he had learned. Unfortunately, Farragut did not take it well. He simply concluded their argument with, "I won't take you there, and for your own safety, I won't tell you the location." Ted shouted about the lives being lost every second. Ted said he can't wait any longer. That pulled the trigger. Farragut bellowed, "Never! didn't I tell you what happened there?" Ted, without waiting, took out his phone and showed pictures of the alarming casualties being lost every second. Farragut glared at the screen, but soon his face was convulsed in horror. California, Jamaica, San Francisco, and many others were burned to the ground; buildings crushed, fires running across the ground, and many other horrors. The army was going to nuke part of the US to erase the infiltrator. Tears welled up in the eyes of many. Death seemed like a hungry child, devouring everything in its path. "Fine," said Farragut, snapping his eyes away from the phone. "Let's go there," he mumbled.

Two weeks was the time period it took them to reach there. The submersible was thoroughly checked and examined by him. At last, while Ted was eating breakfast, Farragut barged in through his room and said it was time to go. Farragut on his way took an old image, which portrays him in his youth with his two companions. They seemed to be full of energy and innocent of what tragedy was going to befall them. Farragut looked at the faces of his companions once more. He didn't seem to have any hopes of returning. Ted was already inside the submersible when Farragut entered it. Farragut simply told Ted that the blue button at his side will eject the submersible back to the ship. The submersible started sinking at the press of a button. It started sinking at a steady pace, neither too fast nor too slow. Ted kept his hand near the blue button, clearly afraid of the expedition. After what seemed like hours, the submersible slowly sank under the water. Farragut seemed surprisingly calm. He seemed to have forgotten that his friends breathed their last in these waters. And so the submersible sank under the darkest waters.

Farragut switched on the lights of the submersible. As the lights beamed, Ted gasped at the sights before him; he seemed to have forgotten that their soul is as good as sealed. Far from the vision of the submersible unnoticed by both of them. There was a movement which sent water rippling. Something was there, something hidden in the dark. Their fate was sealed.

> *"The future is as dark as unreal as the past."*
>
> *– John Gardener*

Chapter 5

The two reached the abyss using the submersible. In the abyss, very few rays of sunlight pierced through the dark waters. Ted remembered that he had once read a book about how creatures living in the abyss attract prey. The creatures, or more appropriately, organisms, use a method called bioluminescence to attract prey because most (almost all creatures living in the abyss) are blind due to very little sunlight. Bioluminescence is basically a light produced by a chemical reaction within a living organism. Bioluminescence is a type of chemiluminescence, which is simply the term for a chemical reaction where light is produced (bioluminescence is chemiluminescence that takes place inside a living organism).

Bioluminescence is basically a "cold light". Cold light means less than 20 percent of the light generates thermal radiation or heat. Most bioluminescent organisms are found in the ocean. These bioluminescent organisms include fish, bacteria, and jellies. Some bioluminescent organisms, including fireflies and fungi, are found on land. There are almost no bioluminescent organisms native to freshwater habitats like lakes, ponds, rivers, etc. Most marine bioluminescence, for instance, is expressed in the blue-green part of the visible light spectrum. These colors are more easily visible in the deep ocean than other colors. Also, most marine organisms are sensitive only to blue-green colors. They are physically unable to process yellow, red, or violet colors. As Ted was remembering facts from the book he had once read, Captain Farragut was sure he saw blue-green light in front of him. He estimated it to be 20 yards away. Even though it was extremely dark, he noticed it. His eyes narrowed. He was not a fool; he knows that some underwater creatures use lights to attract prey. He switched off the light of the submersible. He knew something deadly was coming their way. He knew it would happen. Farragut had installed an electrically unstable device on his submersible. The device was capable of sending current throughout the exterior shell of the submersible. Of course, it would even destroy the submersible, but Farragut was prepared to sacrifice in order to get revenge.

"The man who seeks revenge digs two graves."

– Ken Kesey

CHAPTER 6

Strong ripples could be felt in the water. Even the submersible lurched a little. Ted, who doesn't know much about underwater expeditions, did not find anything amiss. However, Farragut knew something was out of order. His sharp eyes had detected a movement some time ago. The darkness was so thick it felt palpable. Then to the sudden fright, Out of the dark, evil red eyes appeared. Ted felt a bone-chilling fear. Blood froze. He did not even have a time to think, when with a thunderous movement, the giant slammed at the submersible. The inner cabin exploded by the sheer force. Ted screamed as the submersible started spinning out of control and fortunately not hitting any underwater rock. Farragut was much quicker to react, pushed a button. A few seconds later, the light started working even though most of them were damaged by the blow. "Oh God," Farragut murmured as the light brought the creature into focus. It resembled a crocodile, but it was no mere creature of the underwater kingdom. It was around 550 feet long, with broken skin, a cracked head, and red glowing eyes. "Demon," muttered Ted; he was clearly beaten up. This thing was using bioluminescence in its eyes to capture its prey in the darkest depths of the deep.

If this same thing was responsible for the doom of Atlantis, then what chance does a submersible have against its wrath? The inscription itself hints that even the creature wrecking America fears this. Its skin seemed to be irregularly broken, while its head seemed to be cracked. Its smell choked Ted; wait, he was not supposed to smell anything, the submersible was supposed to be sealed unless there is a leak. Ted silently cursed. Farragut managed to brace himself and withstand the force. The lights again switched off by an mechanical error. Farragut switched on the light, but he wished he hadn't. Farragut was taken aback when the light shone on the monster right before their submersible and snarling.

Farragut was breathing heavily. In the distance, he saw the light source which he had seen before.

His friends had told him that the light source marked the remains of Atlantis. He knew that the object which Ted was searching for is that light source. But now stands a Jurassic period creature between them and the object. A thought came into his mind. Farragut remembered the device he installed. He knew that the device was his only hope. Just then the creature decided not to wait and came barreling toward their submersible. It landed a devastating blow on the rattling vehicle. Leakage increased. The submersible was sinking fast. Ted was heavily injured. He groaned. Farragut rushed toward his trigger box and changed the frequencies to activate the device. The device started humming steadily with a red light glowing on it. The outer shell is charged. The creature decided to bite the submersible with its teeth. But the second the teeth dug into the submersible, the high voltage charge flowed into its head. Its eyes widened. The creature let go of the submersible and barreled toward the dark at an alarming speed. Farragut knew that the submersible was heavily damaged and the creature will return soon after the pain subsides. He rushed to Ted and helped him to his feet. He made Ted sit on the ejection pod and pulled the submersible at full speed toward the light source. The engines of the submersible coughed and gave their last force, pushing the submersible toward the light source. He himself was beaten up, but he shrugged his pain off.

As the submersible reached Atlantis, he saw the ruins of Atlantis. He saw three irregularly broken circles with a huge perimeter. He saw traces of Greek and Egyptian architecture. The light source seemed small yet brighter than anything created by humans. Meanwhile, the water had already partially filled the submersible. Farragut saw the volcano of

Atlantis, ever spewing lava. He pushed a button to activate the grabber of the submersible. But that didn't work. The creature would have damaged it. He took a deep breath and swam toward the bottom of the submersible and kicked open a door. Bubbles gushed out. The waterproof motor of the grabber or mechanical hand was present there. He pulled down the emergency lever and swam back to the control room. Water had already filled 75 percent. Farragut took control of a lever and used the grabber to get that light source. By the time the light source came to the control room, water already filled 92 percent. The light source was none other than a scepter with ancient engravings. The middle cylindrical part of the scepter seemed to be responsible for the light. Farragut grabbed it and rushed to the ejection pod. Ted was unconscious. Farragut strapped Ted properly and then did the same to himself, Farragut ejected himself and Ted toward their ship. He knew the monster cannot come into the light. Its eyes were not specialized for that. Farragut relaxed for a bit and closed his eyes.

"To defeat a monster
I had to become one."

– Keri Lake

CHAPTER 7

Farragut and Ted were roughly woken up. A man in a black shirt with a bald head was pulling them. Meanwhile, men with similar identities took the scepter. "Hey, who are you?" asked Ted. The man smiled and gave Ted a punch on his face, rendering Ted unconscious again. Farragut tried to put up a fight but was already weakened. Both of them were handcuffed and carried to their ship. The ship had a really bad aura. When you entered it, you would feel hopeless under the glare of the red light. Even the bold Farragut seemed to fall into the realm of hopelessness. The men weren't kind; they did not answer any of their questions and acted as if Ted and Farragut didn't exist at all. But Ted knew that something was wrong. Farragut tried to fight them and protest as much as he could, but the men were far stronger. The ship seemed to be divided into 2 parts. One was given normal white light while the other part seemed to have red light. Ted and Farragut now stood in front of an iron cell. Both were forcefully pushed inside it and locked. Ted shouted, but nothing happened.

After 2 days:

The 2 days felt like 2 months. Stuck inside that prison, with water and food coming from a small and rectangular hole on the door. They sent barely enough food. It was the worst nightmare of Ted. He was sure he was going to break soon. For now, all he can do is request more food. The big burly men were amused by their pitiful state. They were making fun of them. Farragut clenched his hands in anger. But it was of no use. Just then, the group heard the door lock being opened with keys. They heard the clicking of keys. The door opened, and a burly man came inside the cell. He took Ted and left without a word. He closed the door behind to prevent any means of escape. The man took Ted toward a big room which had a fluorescent yellow light. A man seated on a rich chair. The man wore a coat and had bushy hair. He smiled generously at Ted and asked Ted whether he knew about antimatter. Floods of memories came rushing into Ted's mind.

In modern physics, antimatter is defined as matter composed of the antiparticles (or partner) of the corresponding particles in ordinary matter. Combining matter and antimatter produces something at large amount:

ENERGY

Combine a gram of matter and antimatter, and the result is an energy release comparable to the atomic explosion of Hiroshima. Antimatter was discovered in 1931, and its existence is universally accepted by the scientific community. This is what Einstein's famous equation $E=mc^2$ states. Here, E is energy in joules (1 kilocalorie = 4200 joules), m is the mass in kilograms, and c is the velocity of light.

For example, converting 1 kilogram of matter into energy. The amount of energy we would have produced is

We know $E=mc^2$

Now m = 1 kg and c = 3 x 10 x 10 x 10 x 10 x 10 x 10 x 10 x 10

Hence E = 1 x (3 x 10 x 10 x 10 x 10 x 10 x 10 x 10 x 10 x 3 x 10 x 10 x 10 x 10 x 10 x 10 x 10 x 10) joules

$= 9 \times 10^{16}$

This is equal to 25 billion units (kWh) of energy, or about 25 terawatt-hours.

The world consumes 20,000 TWh of electricity in a year. If we destroy 400 kilograms of matter by mixing it with exactly 400 kilograms of antimatter, it would supply the whole world with all the power it needs for a full year. Ted had learned this when he read a book about the famous equation:

$E = mc^2$.

Such were the memories filling his mind.

"I see you have brought 60,000 milligrams of antimatter with you," said the leader tauntingly.

A lump of fear mixed with excitement formed in Ted's throat. Ted gasped in shock; he never thought he would find antimatter. He can change the world with his amazing discovery. A new source of energy, a reduction in electricity, it all could be possible. But it also had a dark side; More powerful weapons, highly advanced warfare. And if such a thing is in the hands of a terrorist (which it is right now), they can threaten world governments. Destroy cities by using a gram of matter and antimatter. That should not happen, thought Ted. "Now, I want you to tell me where you found it and if there is more in that place," the leader continued. "Why should I?" asked Ted rudely. The man laughed and said, "If you don't, then that old man will have to suffer." "Atlantis," whispered in fear of his companion being killed. The leader threw back his head and laughed. "You seriously thought I will keep my word," snorted the leader. "Kill his companion when we arrive at the port," commanded the leader. The big burly man took the protesting Ted away from the leader. As Ted was taken away he observed a Abbreviation-A.W.G

"*If you had the power to destroy the world, would you do so?*"

– Bertrand Russel

Chapter 8

Ted was devastated; he had failed to protect his companion. He should not have believed the leader's word. He felt miserable in his tiny iron cell. Then he heard the voice of a big burly man, "Giddy up, we're goanna reach Yemen. Master has some old friends in Yemen." Farragut was angry and worried, angry at realizing how bad their expedition ended up and worried about what had happened to Ted. Farragut was shouting and protesting at the big burly man, but he just laughed in response. Ted wanted to tell Farragut that it was hopeless, but he didn't want to shatter his friend's hope. Suddenly, the ship stopped and shuddered. The big burly man took a key from his belt and opened the lock of the cell. The lock clicked and opened. The big burly man led them toward their exit. They exited the ship and felt freedom from their cell. Never had they appreciated the soft breeze; now, both felt thankful. Ted exited from the ship but was immediately stopped by the snarling man. Then a private van, black and white striped, stopped right in front of them; the men loaded them inside like loading luggage. They closed the door, and the van sped off. Captain Farragut felt lost. Recently, he had to defeat a Jurassic era monster and find the most prized possession of a fallen kingdom. At those times, he felt like a hero, but only to be caught by a terrorist gang and made helpless. What would have happened to him if he didn't try to find Atlantis in the first place? Would he be sailing toward home? Will his friends still be alive? No one can tell for sure. The van stopped without warning. As they jumped out of the van, they saw a big board with the words "ADEN INT'L AIRPORT." They passed through all the security and reached a runway, where a small private plane was parked. Farragut had taken a small stone when he was a prisoner and sharpened it.

Suddenly, he lunged forward and made a deep cut in the arm of a big burly man, who was leading them, and shouted, "Now! Get in the plane." Ted, out of fear, quickly went into the plane. Farragut, meanwhile, was doing a great job keeping them at bay. Thankfully, due to security purposes, those guys couldn't get their guns with them. Moments later, Farragut barged in, clearly beaten up and injured. "What are we going to do?" asked Ted without any plan. Farragut said that he knew how to handle a plane. When Ted asked how, he just grunted. Farragut had 10 minutes to get the plane in the air before the military stormed in. Farragut was fiddling with buttons and levers. Ted saw some jeeps with military men holding guns come closer to the plane. "Hurry up," said Ted in a panicked tone. There was a radio transmission asking them to surrender. The military then gave the orders to fire on the plane. Just then, Farragut started the engines, and the plane started to move at a steadily increasing speed. Right on cue, a bullet pierced the side of the plane. "Move it on, move it on," Farragut was clearly struggling. Ted ducked to avoid the bullets from grazing his head. A song or, more appropriately, a poem came into his mind.

"There are dark days and stormy, which come to us all,

When about us in ruin, our hopes seem to fall.

But stand by whatever you happen to meet –

We must all drink the bitter as well as the sweet.

And the test of your courage is: what do you do?

In the hour when reverses are coming to you.

Never changed is the battle by curse or regret,

Though you whimper and whine, still the end must be met

And who fights a good fight, though in a struggle in vain,

Shall have many a victory to pay for his pain.

So take your reverses as part of the plan.

Which God has devised for creating a man?"

The poem, or rather stanzas, played in Ted's mind continuously like a song from a broken radio.

Meanwhile, the plane rose higher and higher in the air, away from the soldiers who were shooting.

Eventually, the place reached a height where the bullets could not reach them.

The gunners were forced to halt.

Ted was sure all the soldiers (including armored jeep drivers) were glaring at them.

If glaring can make an object burn, the plane would have been toast by now.

"Where to?" asked Farragut, with a bored face as if nothing terrifying had happened.

"I am Googling." said Ted.

The plane headed for its next adventure.

> *"It's time for a new adventure."*
>
> *– Linsey Miller*

Chapter 9

A voice came over the plane's communication system: "This is the Air Force of Taizz. Identify yourselves."

Behind them, a dark silhouette of a jet arose.

"What should we do?" whispered Ted.

"What else, hope for the best and prepare for the worst.

For a moment, there was silence, both dreading the worst possible outcomes.

Then the voice decided to break the silence.

"Identify your selves," repeated the AI voice.

Ted looked at Farragut, who nodded.

The voice once again decided to break the tension.

"Identify yourselves."

Farragut proceeded to land the plane. He told Ted to brace up. Farragut pulled a lever and started pressing some buttons.

The plane descended.

"Land on lane 14b," instructed the voice. The LEDs around lane 14b began to glow.

The plane continued on its steady descent. The plane came closer and closer to the lane. A hatch on the underneath of the plane opened. Two wheels came out steadily. The panels of the plane's wing rattled. The plane's system was reporting their current distance.

'20 meters above ground level' '10 meters above ground level'

The plane's wheel scratched the lane at last. The plane shuddered on contact with the ground. Ted stumbled. The plane moved at terrific speed. But then after some minutes, it started slowing down steadily. Soon, the plane came to a stop. Farragut had made a reasonably smooth landing.

"Now, the tough part," Farragut mumbled and pressed a button as the door began to open.

The two walked toward the door. The door began to open. The rays of sunlight appeared on the floor of the plane. Ted and Farragut raised their arms in surrender. As they reached the door, a fearful sight awaited them. Loads of soldiers were circled around the plane with their rifles ready. More than a dozen army jeeps were circled around them. Ted raised his arms in surrender. Farragut arrogantly hesitated, but then followed suit. A man, clad in a military uniform, gestured for them to follow him.

"For all of its uncertainty, we cannot flee the future."

— Barbara Jordan

Chapter 10

The airport was buzzing with people. They did not enter the airport but a small building near it. The building was gray in color. It had only 5 windows. Even more the building seemed like a symbol of strictness. The gate had 5 layers of grill.

It took the soldier 10 minutes to unlock the gate. Then he threw back the locks and opened the grills. Then he gestured for them to get inside.

They entered without hesitation. There were no extra rooms, only a big hall. Two huge staircases led up to a pavement. One side of the pavement was grilled, while on the other side were cells with grilled gates. In the hall, there was a table; the table had one chair on one side and six on the other sides.

The man gestured for them to sit in the chairs. Ted sat down, while Farragut on the other hand who hesitated a little. The man gestured again. Farragut reluctantly sat down on the chair. The man said a simple word, "confess".

Ted blurted out everything. The man's piercing but calm look made Ted confess without hesitation and lies. It took them 1 hour to explain it. The man didn't even utter a single word while they talked. After they talked, the man said two simple words: "nice joke". He even chuckled a little. "You don't believe us?" asked Ted in a surprised tone. "You guys say that you discovered a mythical kingdom, a terrorist organization and a creature which is supposed to be dead for more than a thousand years," sneered the man. For a brief moment, there was only silence. "However, there might be a possibility that the organization exists," the man continued. "So, you do believe us," Ted said with a renewed hope.

'"I said there might be," said the man with a smile. "Now, I need to check the database to find if A.W.G exists." With that, he went toward the door and closed it, leaving them to be shut off from nature.'

After what seemed like 5 hours, the man returned. He was silent for a long time, carefully observing them with eyes like an eagle. His sharp eyes detected even the smallest movements. Finally, he broke the curtain of silence which hung over them by saying that there was indeed a terrorist group like that in the database. He also said that they would be deploying the captain who is closest to the place. However, he said if the place doesn't exist, you would be in highly serious trouble. With that, the man gestured to an officer to give them food and left the room.

Atlantic Ocean:

Captain Bluebeard's wistful eyes gazed into the vast emptiness of the great sea. His body clearly showed his premature aging. He wore a regular navy uniform. His beard, which should have been black, turned white due to his stress. His map was never left alone by his hands. He had just received an order from his higher officials. He had been in this field for more than 20 years. He sighed and strode back to the main room. The men were laughing and having a private joke. He casually asked a single question, "How near are we to the coordinates?" His strong voice spoke of authority. His commanding tone made the men flinch and immediately answer the question as if their life depended on it. The captain nodded grimly. Suddenly, the alarms flashed red. The radar also flashed red, detecting 5 objects coming near it. The captain looked out of the window and his sharp eyes detected what looked like a periscope. "Arm the guns," he ordered. "On my command, fire!" the captain bellowed. The captain sent a warning transmission to the submarine.

The submarine captain was devastated. "How did they find our greatest secret?" his mind wondered.

"Send the torpedoes," he muttered. "What?" asked one of his men. "I said send the torpedoes!" the captain bellowed at the top of his voice. The man showed the barest hint of hesitation but ran toward the ammunition room to carry out his boss's order.

Captain Bluebeard had underestimated their potential. But all he could do now was gaze at the impending doom. "Fire!" the captain bellowed in a desperate act to defend the ship with its own torpedoes. The ship shuddered as the weapons of mass destruction were launched. The floorboards rattled. The men counted when it would hit the incoming torpedoes sent by the enemies. "three, two, and one," the man screamed, just as the torpedoes clashed. The ship shook and shuddered to its core. Men were flying and shouting, while some managed to dexterously hold the railing.

The situation on the enemy submarine was not much better. The powerful blast had sent the submarine spinning toward an underwater rock. "Brace for impact," the captain bellowed. "On 3, 2, 1," he shouted as the submarine hit the rock with an almighty force. The submarine started vibrating. The teeth of the men and the captain rattled. The captain stood up and asked about the status of the submarine. He moved toward the communication desk and sent a transmission of surrender.

Captain Bluebeard was the first person to notice the incoming transmission. He asked the crew to brace up and be in their positions. He knew the risk that the transmission might be a trick. But he asked the crew of the enemy submarine to board the ship of Captain Bluebeard and be handcuffed by Captain Bluebeard's crew. Captain Bluebeard looked at the sky and muttered a famous quote from Herman Melville.

"Consider the subtleness of the sea; how its most dreaded creatures glide under water, unapparent for the most part, and treacherously hidden beneath the loveliest tints of azure."

– Herman Melville

CHAPTER 11

Hell was the only thing that crossed their minds as they were trapped in the unforgivable building. Even after eating food, they felt like they were starving. Sleep deprivation was hitting them hard now. They didn't even know how long they had been trapped in the building and how long they would be trapped.

After what seemed like days, they heard the hopeful sound of the locks being unlocked. A man stepped in and gazed at them, and with another of his artistic gestures, he gestured for them to follow him. Bright and vibrant sunlight beamed on their faces. They partially closed their eyes to protect them.

The airport was as crowded and buzzing as ever. People were running and laughing about their hopeful vacations. The man and they seemed like they were walking like a few goats in a huge flock of sheep. People saw them and exchanged curious glances.

The man led them to a police van and gestured for them to enter. They sat without showing even the barest hint of hesitation. Just like the people buzzing in the airport, questions were buzzing in their minds. The man closed the van door. The van had a really bad odor. The van's inside was brown, and it had some torn seats. The van, in simple words, stank. The van's cabin was divided in two by a metal grill. The driver was a cop. He did not speak English but spoke to the man, whose name was Captain Amon as they had known from the previous confrontations with him, in a language which the Ted failed to recognize. Captain Amon sat next to the cop and motioned for him to start the van. The two noticed that Captain Atom was a man who loves and favors signing and gesturing. The cop started the van. The van's engine coughed and spluttered. At first, the van lurched back, and then it took off at a terrific speed. The windows were closed and opaque, giving them no view of the outside. They could only see the outside through the windshield.

Soon they reached a highway. There were lots of speed limit signs along the side of the wide road. Finally, the brakes were pressed, and the tires squeaked, lurching the van to a stop. Captain Amon opened the door and stepped out of the van. He went toward the back doors and opened them, letting them all out. They nearly stumbled as they emerged from the bad-smelling and, in a way, torturous van. They sighed and contentedly breathed in the sweet scent of fresh air. The cop drove his van away. They were standing in front of a thin but tall building. It had a rather twisting shape. The building was painted silver, with very few windows. In front of it, there was a lawn and a circular road with a beautiful fountain in the middle, depicting a white statue of an angel. The angel had wings and was holding a scepter with a coiled rod and an orb at the top. The statue was larger than life-size.

Again, Captain Amon used one of his somewhat irritating gestures to call them toward the building. The doors were open for them. The inside of the building was air-conditioned. There were many floors. The building was built with a modern style. There were lots of separate cabins and computers of cutting-edge tech. However, there were only two people inside the building. One was a woman, while the other was a man. Both were wearing the same uniform. It read Egyptian Archaeological and Scientific Research Department. One smiled while the other glared.

Atlantic Ocean:

Captain Bluebeard's men were working as fast as they could. The captain of the enemy ship, Wilbert, was forced to surrender with his accomplices.

Captain Bluebeard was strolling on the enemy submarine when he noticed a vault. He asked his assistant, Jennifer, to bring Captain Wilbert. Captain Bluebeard, while waiting, studied the vault. It was round and seemed to be made of steel; however, it was painted brown to match the interior of the submarine. It had bronze knobs, and hinges of steel. Jennifer arrived with the handcuffed Captain Wilbert. "Open," ordered Captain Bluebeard in a proud, superior, and commanding tone. The helpless captain reluctantly set the timer and pulled it open. Jennifer stifled a gasp. Captain Bluebeard stared at it open-mouthed. Inside the vault, there was a glowing scepter, far brighter than any man-made objects, which was found on Atlantis.

"What is it?" asked Jennifer.

"Some kind of hyper energy source," whispered Captain Bluebeard. Gone was his commanding tone. In its place, there was a bewildered tone.

"Where did you find it?" asked Captain Bluebeard.

"Oh, you wouldn't believe me if I told you," said Wilbert in a soft tone, grinning for the first time that day. He was openly savoring their bewilderment.

"Tell," commanded Captain Bluebeard, regaining his bold voice.

"Atlantis," said Wilbert slowly and theatrically, raising his handcuffed hands.

Minutes later:

"Set course for the coordinates I gave you," bellowed Captain Bluebeard. His thirst for adventure was burning more than ever. He remembered a really short discussion between Professor Arronax and Captain Nemo from 20,000 Leagues Under the Sea written by Jules Verne:

"Professor Arronax: "Your dead sleep quietly, at least, Captain, out of the reach of sharks."

"Captain Nemo: "Yes, sir, of sharks and Men."

Jules Verne

This might as well be referring to Atlantis. The Atlanteans' dead remains were buried under the ocean, for centuries they were in their eternal sleep out of the reach of men.

"Not for long," thought Captain Bluebeard. "Soon, they will be under the reach of men," thought Captain Bluebeard. "Not for long."

"Long before the advent of what scientists and scholars consider to be the beginning of human civilization, there was an age undreamed of... the age of Atlantis."

– Frederick Lenz

PART 2

CHAPTER 12

The man's name was Badru. The woman's name was Bahiti. They were from the Egyptian Archaeological and Scientific Research Department. They dealt with works related to discoveries and excavations of many tombs and pyramids in Egypt. They took them on a tour along the building. There were also everyday objects of ancient Egypt ranging from ivory headrests to scribing tools. It was like a huge museum of ancient Egypt. All this while they didn't even utter a single word. The ancient Egyptians always drew only one side of humans because they were scared that if they drew the full body, the drawing would come alive. At last, they reached the elevator. They pressed the up arrow button.. They waited for some moments until the elevator came to their level. The iron doors opened slowly, and they went inside. The elevator was very spacious. It looked like it could hold fifteen people at a single time. The elevator had buttons of floors till the eighth floor and an emergency alarm button. Badru pushed the seventh-floor button. The doors slowly closed in. The elevator ascended at a slow but increasing speed.

After one or two minutes, the elevator reached the seventh floor. The elevator's, obviously, electric doors opened slowly with the joyous sound of a bell ringing. The elevator opened into a shockingly clean corridor. The tiles were neatly polished and shining. The overhead circle of very bright LED lights made the tiles glisten. The corridor was irregularly curved, somewhat resembling a circle shape. It had many doors. Each seemed to lead to a meeting hall. They walked toward one such room. The door was plain white with no designs. It had a rectangular two-way mirror in the center of it. The door had a keyhole and it was locked. Badru took a key from his shirt pocket and inserted it into the keyhole. The key went in with a soft click. He turned the key clockwise. The door clicked open as the lock was released. Bahiti opened the white door smoothly and gestured for them to go inside. Inside, it was fully air-conditioned. It was so cool that Ted shivered. The room was so big. There were around twenty chairs. Each person occupied one chair (of course, each only occupied one chair; otherwise, it would have been weird to see one person sitting on 2 chairs). "Now," began Badru. "We have applied for your return to home, but ……" He said. "Except

Ted," finished Bahiti. "Why?" Farragut asked at the same time. "Because he is an archaeologist," growled Badru. "Calm down and rest for a while," said Bahiti. "I know what to do," snapped the frightfully angry man. "I have an idea," said Bahiti, "Why don't you wait in the next room?" Farragut went out of the room. Only Badru, Ted, and Bahiti remained in the room.

"Now, how did you" before Badru could finish his phone interrupted him. "One sec," he said and answered his phone. "Hello, what the heck!" shouted a bewildered Badru. "It can't be," he whispered. "What?" asked Bahiti. "Anti," whispered Badru. "What?" asked Bahiti easily. "Mater," snapped Badru. "What matter?" asked Bahiti. "Antimatter!" screamed the frightfully angry man. Ted snorted with laughter.

A simple glare from Badru cut off his laughter. Bahiti regained her posture. "Now," said Badru. "It has been proved that what you claim is true; antimatter exists," said Badru. Ted gave his best 'told you so' look. "What did it say?" asked Bahiti. "What did who say?" asked Ted. "The inscription," gritted Bahiti. "Oh, wait," Ted strained to remember what it had said. "Oh, I got it -

"To defeat Chronos, the monster, hunt the weapon of gods which holds the power to unite the heavens and

hell; Find it in the land which lost its right on land and was swallowed by an ocean of despair, but remember what sunk the kingdom was not only a monster, but a being equal to a hundred monsters, so terrifying the true demon is, that the name of it is untold and its true boundaries are the shackles which chain it to water, unable to set foot on land. Find Hunahpu and conquer DEIMOS.

Now the second lies with the oracle of Apollo, the Cancer shows it. Remember the hero's oath; find the three, older than rocks. Find Xbalanque and conquer Phobos. And then you may conquer war itself."

Ted looked at their faces. They had unreadable expressions. "Now we need to find who or what Xbalanque and Hunahpu are," said Bahiti. She took her phone and typed them into the web. "I got something," she said and started reading.

> *"Become a legend and make your existence worth remembering."*
>
> *– Anonymous*

CHAPTER 13

In the darkness before creation was complete, the gods sent a great flood that wiped out humanity. In this time of darkness, twins named One and Seven Hunahpu were born.

These boys were great ball players. They were working out in their ball court when messengers arrived from the Lords of Death. "The Lords of Death want you to come play ball with them in Xibalba," said the messengers. They set out for Xibalba, the kingdom of the Lords of Death. And when they came to Xibalba, approaching the throne room of the Lords of Death, they greeted them cheerfully by name. Only these weren't the Lords of Death at all, but just carved wooden replicas.

The real Lords of Death laughed hysterically. The Lords asked them to relax on a bench. Only the bench was scorching hot. The Lords convulsed in laughter once more. The Lords asked them to go to their rooms and rest. They promised to give them cigars and torches.

So when they went to their bedroom, the torch and cigars were brought. "You'll have to give these back in the morning," the twins were told. But the cigars were already lit, so they smoked them. And in the morning the Lords of Death weren't pleased. The Lords were angry and killed them.

Their bodies were buried under the ballcourt, there in Xibalba. But the head of one Hunahpu was placed in the form of a calabash tree. The tree bore fruit, and it was impossible to distinguish the head of one Hunahpu from the calabashes.

The tree was put off-limits by the Lords of Death, but a maiden named Blood Woman heard that its fruit was sweet. She couldn't see why it should wither and die untested. So she approached the tree.

The head of one Hunahpu spat into her palm. The head told her to leave Xibalba and go to the land of the living. The frightened woman did so. And the saliva of one Hunahpu grew into twin babies in the womb of the maiden Blood Woman. And her father, seeing she was with child, betrayed her to the Lords of Death. The Lords of Death demanded the name of the father. The poor woman was confused.

They asked the owls to bring the heart of the woman. However, she convinced them and managed to trick the Lords of Death.

She went to the house of her mother-in-law and gave birth to the second hero twins. They were named Hunahpu and Xbalanque.

Now the twins decided to make a garden. While doing so, they caught a rat. They held his tail over the fire. They choked him. They were starting to kill him when the rat protested, talking fast to save his hide. The rat advised them to quit gardening and told them about their heritage.

And the next day, they were playing ball like their fathers before them. They had a boisterous time of it. Their gleeful shouts and the thud of the hard rubber ball on their pads were heard down below in Xibalba. The Lords of Death were angered. "They're no more humble than their fathers. It's not right that they should show such prowess. Bring them here; we'll give them a game."

And so messengers were dispatched, but when they arrived at the house in the clearing, the boys weren't there. They were still off playing ball. The messengers then spoke to the grandmother, giving her the summons to be relayed. It broke her heart to think that she would lose her grandsons to the Lords of Death, just as she had lost her sons before them.

But Xbalanque and Hunahpu did not hesitate when they heard the call. Down they went to

Xibalba. Scaling the cliff, they came to the rivers of blood and pus. They didn't just wade in. Instead, they used their blowgun like a canoe. When they came to the Crossroads, they knew which road to take. But they also knew that the Lords of Death expected to be greeted by name. Indeed, this was a test, a trial.

So Hunahpu plucked a hair from his shin, and it turned into a mosquito. The mosquito went on ahead and bit the first Lord of Death. However, there was no reaction, for this was no real Lord, but a wooden replica. Now the twins wouldn't fall for that trick. The mosquito bit the next Lord, still no reaction. But when it bit the next in line, he let out a cry. "What's the matter, Pus Master?" asked the one seated next to him.

'Something bit me,' said Pus Master, and now the twins knew his name. And when the mosquito bit the other Lords and each cried out in turn, the twins learned all the names. Then up they strode and entered the throne room of Xibalba. 'We're not saying good morning to wooden dummies,' they said. But the real Lords of Death they greeted properly, and they greeted them by name. They had passed the first test. The Lords of Death gritted their teeth in frustration.

The boys said that they would not sit on the scorching chair. And thus, they saved their behinds. The Lords of Death did not argue. These were just the first tests. There were many others in store, starting with the cigars and torch gag. "Return these in the morning just like you got them," the twins were told when they were escorted to their chamber and handed the burning torch and the pre-lit cigars. But Xbalanque and Hunahpu knew better than to let the torch burn out. Instead, they swapped a macaw's scarlet tail feathers for the flame. And they stuck fireflies on the ends of their cigars.

"Who are these two?" demanded the Lords of Death when the items were returned the next morning. "They look just like those other twins, but they're getting the better of us. Not to worry, though, when we play ball it's our ballcourt and our ball." And this ball wasn't a ball at all, but a dagger shaped like a sphere.

The Lords took a shot, but Hunahpu blocked it. The dagger was exposed from inside the ball.

Now they played with the plain rubber ball supplied by the boys. It was a close match. The teams were about equal in strength and skill, but the twins had the advantage of thinking pure thoughts. In the end, though, they allowed themselves to be defeated.

For the prize, the Lords of Death asked for many colored flowers.

And knowing that the only flowers in Xibalba were in their own garden, the Lords of Death warned their guardians, "Keep a good eye out tonight. Those boys will surely make a raid." But those guardian birds were singularly oblivious.

The boys were sent first to the Razor House, where sharp blades were to cut them to pieces. But they convinced the blades that their job was to cut up animals, not hero twins, and the blades let them be. Now they called all the ants of Xibalba to do them a favor.

"Go to the garden and cut some flowers for us," they said.

And the ants did as they were told. They cut the flowers right under the noses of the guardian birds. The Lords of Death didn't look too happy when they received their prize.

A night game was played. It was a tie. They agreed to play again in the morning. The boys were sent to the Bat House. The Bat House they survived by hiding inside their blowgun, while the razor-like teeth of the giant bats gnashed through the night.

Now they made a mistake, but they did it on purpose. Hunahpu decided to peek outside the blowgun and see if it was morning yet. When he did so, a bat sliced off his head, and it went rolling out onto the ballcourt.

Xbalanque cried out as if he had given up hope. But he called all the animals together, asking each to bring its favorite food. The coati brought a squash, and with the help of the gods this became a new head for Hunahpu.

The Lords of Death started the game, using Hunahpu's head for the ball. As far as they were concerned, this made them victors automatically. But Hunahpu dared them to kick the ball, and they took the dare. Xbalanque deflected the shot and then sent Hunahpu's head flying toward the rabbit's hiding place. The rabbit hopped off; the Lord of Death thought it was the bouncing ball, and they raced off in pursuit, baying like hounds.

The boys got Hunahpu's head back and put the squash in its place. "It's right here!" they shouted to the Lords of Death.

"How did we miss it?" they asked, looking foolish. "Who cares? Play ball!"

Now the game was played in earnest, only the ball wasn't up to it. When Xbalanque gave it a particularly energetic boot, it split open and all its seeds came spilling out. The hero twins had defeated the Lords of Xibalba.

So the Lords of Death, with all their tricks and all their tests, couldn't kill the hero twins. But still, the boys knew that they would have to die for their quest to be complete. They even knew how the Lords of Death would kill them. So when they were called before the Lords of Xibalba and challenged to a new and different game, they knew it was a trick. "See this oven?" said the Lords of Death. "Bet you can't jump over it 4 times."

"We're not falling for that one," said the boys, and without any further ado, they jumped right into the flames. The Lords of Death were beside themselves with exultation. At this point, they made a big mistake. Instead of throwing Xbalanque and Hunahpu over a cliff or hanging their bodies in a tree, they ground their bones on a grinding stone and sprinkled them in the river. This was the only way that the twins could come back to life. And come back they did, first as catfish and then as their normal selves.

Only now their outward appearance was different. They looked like tattered beggars, the kind who go about dancing and performing tricks for a living. And their tricks were quite amazing. They'd burn a house down and then make it like new. They'd even sacrifice each other, laying down under the blade then springing up again. Word of their renown reached the Lords of Death, and they were summoned for a command performance.

Xbalanque dismembered his twin and cut out his heart. Then he started dancing and commanded Hunahpu to get up and join him. And when Hunahpu got up as good as new, the Lords of Death were caught up in a frenzy of delight.

"Now do us!" they cried. And so the twins sacrificed the two foremost of the Lords of Death. Only they didn't bring them back to life. And the other Lords knew that they had been defeated, and from that day forth Xibalba had lost its glory.

> *"But man by his nature is an unnatural animal.*
> *If any creature stands a chance of defeating death, it is man."*
>
> *— Tom Robbins*

CHAPTER 14

"Useless," said Badru after hearing the story."

"Not entirely, it might help in the future," said Bahiti.

"Leave it," said Ted. "We already found the first part 'Hunahpu' in Atlantis, so let's go for other lines," Ted continued.

"'Now the second lies in with the oracle of Apollo, the Cancer shows it. Remember the hero's oath, find the three, older than rocks. Find Xbalanque and conquer Phobos. And then you may conquer war itself.'"

"Interesting," murmured Badru. "Well, we already know about the oracles and their locations, but what about this Cancer?" wondered Badru.

"Well, it's definitely not the disease," said Ted.

"Of course, I knew that," snapped Badru.

'It might be the constellation Cancer,' said Bahiti.

"You must be correct," said Badru.

"But what about the oracles?" asked Bahiti.

"They are and must be related to Greek mythology. They say the words of Lord Apollo. But the thing is they give hints about people and people won't understand it till it occurs," explained Ted.

'But we are looking for a location, we don't need what they do,' said Badru.

'Of course,' said Ted. He opened his phone and typed the location of the oracles in the web browser.

"There are 5 main temples where the oracles lived. Here they are," Ted showed them the image that appeared on the browser of his phone.

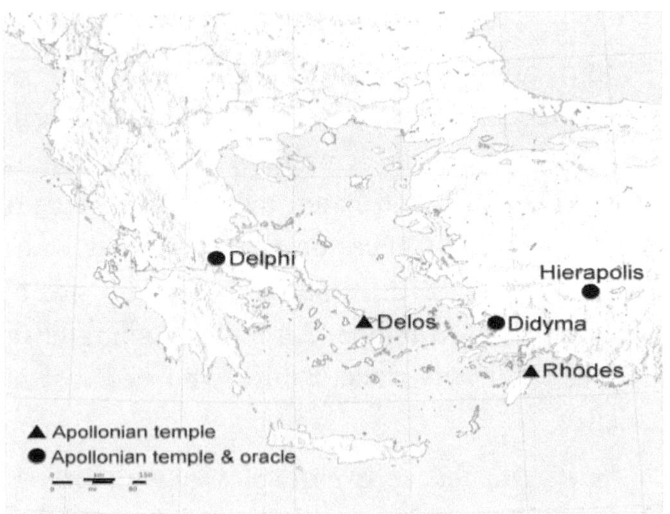

"It must be one of them," concluded Badru.

"Well, we can't just go and check all of it. It might take lots of time, and we don't exactly have time," said Bahiti.

"Oh no," whispered Ted in a tone of unspeakable horror. A notification had arrived on his phone. The object had destroyed an entire part of America; the army's efforts on a nuclear attack had failed, and it was attacking all the countries of America. He showed it to the others, who visibly gasped in shock.

"We need to concentrate, otherwise it will be useless," spoke Badru. Ted nodded.

"There is no need for us to check all the places," said Ted. "They have given us a hint about Cancer."

"But how could it be? Hold it," Ted had interrupted Badru. Badru simply glared. Ted again took the photo of the Temples of the Oracle on his phone. Then he asked Badru to show the image of the constellation Cancer on Badru's phone. Badru did so. Ted took Badru's phone and held it side by side with his own phone. An understanding lit up his face. "What?" asked Bahiti, who had lost all patience.

"See," said Ted, apparently pleased with himself.

Bahiti was the one who understood it first. She gasped.

Badri tried to figure out what was happening.

Bahiti looked at the resemblance that lay before her.

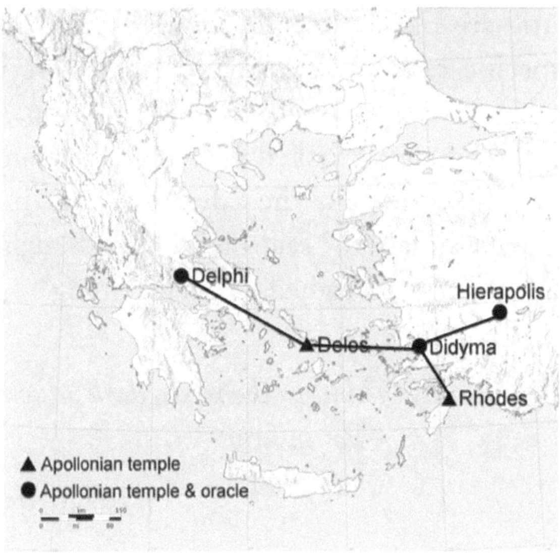

"I can't see the resemblance," confessed Badru.

"Join the temples of Apollo," instructed Ted. Badru did so. "Oh, I see it," exclaimed Badru in excitement.

"But it isn't perfect," said Bahiti. "Why?" asked Ted. "Because if you tilt the constellation at the same angle of the map, then the temple Delphi should be at a much lower position than its current location," explained Bahiti. "You are right, but perhaps it would have been a geographical mistake," mused Ted. "No, it can't be. These people built all these temples with approximate perfection and precision except for one. It can't be a mere mistake unless," spoke Badru. "Unless what?" asked Ted urgently. Badru's eyes lit up. "Unless they are trying to mark that specific temple alone," exclaimed Badru.

"You are right, after all, we are trying to find the specific temple!" exclaimed Bahiti. "We must prepare for a flight," said Badru. "Hold on, what about the Farragut?" asked Ted. "Farragut can stay here at the lodge, it is the safest place for him in the current situation," said Badru. Ted thought for a moment and then sighed, "Lets get going".

> *"His old life lay behind in the mists, dark adventure lies in front."*
>
> *– J.R.R. Tolkien*

CHAPTER 15

It was time for goodbye. It had been three days since they guessed the location of the second antimatter tube. They had arranged for a flight to central Greece. Ted had packed his things in a suitcase, which they had been generously offered. While packing, he thought about the day he packed things in Florida. At that time, he never would have even thought about the adventures it led to in his wildest dreams. But, here he was trying to find something which was believed to have been destroyed in the Big Bang according to the Big Bang theory (obviously).

At present, he was walking toward the entrance with his suitcase. He had concern and worry about Farragut's safety, not that anyone could harm him. But Badru had promised him he would be safe. Ever since he had started this adventure, he had a lingering thought of missing his home in Florida. at the back of his mind. After all, there is no place like home. He was also worried about his families safety. And he wasn't allowed by the government to call to them yet. So for them, he was as good as dead and considered one of the victims of "The Golden Wind Tragedy".

Ted sighed. He got into the taxi that was allotted for them. The taxi engine roared, and it started moving. Ted looked back at the building and said, "au revoir" (goodbye in French).

An Hour Later:

The taxi arrived at the airport. A huge TV was flashing news about the drone attacking San Francisco.

Badru led the way. It took them half an hour to get through the checking.

At last, they were fully checked and allowed to board the plane. It was a private plane. The model was a Gulfstream G450.

(The Gulfstream 450 can climb to 41,000 feet in 23 minutes. After more than 800 hours of wind tunnel testing and aerodynamic improvements, the

Gulfstream 450 is able to cruise at 0.85 Mach (476 knots) while at a cruise altitude of 41,000 feet. The Gulfstream 450's flight envelope extends up to 45,000 feet.)

The trio sat on the comfortable seats. The powerful Tay Mk 611-8c engines of the Gulfstream 450 whirred into motion.

The pilot said some words about safety precautions. The beast of a plane started moving. It was gaining a momentum in speed. Their surroundings were starting to turn into a blur. The plane was slowly gaining an increase in altitude. In the next few moments, the plane was completely in the air. The heavens of the skies were less cloudy and warm, ideal for flying. It was a majestic sight to behold.

Inside the aircraft, there was a veil of silence. The veil was impenetrable. Each had their own concerns and worries. Each was drowning in their own irresistible seas of thoughts. The plane went on a journey. It could be the start of the end.

"Now this is not the end. It is not even the beginning of the end. But it is, perhaps, the end of the beginning."

Winston Churchill, The Lord Mayor's Luncheon, Mansion House, 10th November 1942

Chapter 16

The Gulfstream landed at Nea Anchialos National Airport. It was around 152.2 km away from Mount Parnassus, where Delphi was located. By the time they arrived it was the starting of a night. A Mercedes Sprinter was waiting for them. It was a 2020 model.

It had a sticker on its door, which said "Sama Egypt Limousine and car rental". It was black and shiny. Even if you searched on its metal body for a whole day, you would not find a speck of dirt on it. Even though there were only four of them, including the driver, there were a total of 15 seats. The powerful engine roared and the van took off.

Ted took his iPad and showed them some images. He first took some images of current Delphi. Then he showed some images of how archaeologists digitally reconstructed Delphi and how it might have looked in the 8th century.

CURRENT DELPHI

DELPHI IN THE 8th CENTURY:

"Lots of it got destroyed," said Badru (proving once and for all that he owned the throne of obviousness).

"Well then, how are we goanna find the antimatter?" asked Bahiti.

"According to Wikipedia, there was this Greek guy Pausanias who says that Delphi had 5 major temples; The first one was created in the form of a hut made from laurels, the second temple was either constructed by beeswax, feathers, or ferns, the third temple was said to be made of bronze, the fourth temple was made of stone, while the fifth temple's information and structure are unknown," said Ted, completely ignoring Bahiti.

"But the picture of Delphi in the image constructed by AI doesn't show any signs that these 5 temples existed," said Bahiti.

"'Exactly, is the image wrong?" asked Badru.'

"No, the image couldn't be wrong," said Ted.

"Then?" asked Badru.

"The temples must be underground," proudly stated Ted while boasting and self-praising himself in his mind.

"Heck, it actually makes sense," said Bahiti as enlightenment crowded her mind.

"But where could it be?" asked Badru with his childlike innocence at the moment.

"Ask AI," said Ted with a big old smirk on his face.

"Eh?" asked an astounded Badru with a look as if final exam had come early.

"Just kidding," said Ted with a playful, childlike smile on his face.

"Uhh, we have arrived," said Bahiti, breaking the scene.

The limousine had landed near a campsite. The trio got off it and walked toward the campsite. There was an old processional path nearby. And they marched into it. It seems that Delphi was about four kilometers from there. But without a hint of complaint, they marched. Since it was a very old path, most of it was broken. It confused them at times as to where they should go, until Badru noticed the circle symbols on some rocks and said that these would have been drawn by the authorities to keep track of the path. With this help, they marched and marched until they reached Delphi. By the end of their march, it was more of a tired, stricken walk than a bold march. Ted had wanted to see the Delphi museum first as it might have some clues.

Soon, they faced a square museum and entered it; the interiors were plain, but the count of artifacts was numerous. But first, Ted got some bad news: the creature had destroyed tons of places in America, and the United Nations had announced a worldwide alert of emergency. Countries are equipping themselves with nuclear weapons. The United Nations had also prepared for an atomic bombing like Hiroshima and Nagasaki on the creature. Ted found this information bone-chilling.

Badru distracted him successfully and asked him whether he could find anything useful for them in the museum. There were rocks shaped like shields, idols, humanoid statues, and mysterious artifacts, but none seemed to have any use for them. Ted spent 2 hours at the museum desperately trying to find something. Alas, nothing could be found. Ted secretly seethed in rage for the time wasted.

"Let's head out for Delphi," said Ted. Soon they walked again, this time to Delphi, where they were sure that the end would begin.

"Today is either the beginning of the end, or the end of the beginning."

– Eckhard Pfeiffer

CHAPTER 17

There wasn't much on Delphi; mostly it was ruins. How they are going to find Xbalanque or the other scepter remained a mystery. Ted wasn't sure whether there is any antimatter lying there. But he should try his best, surely. So Badru ordered everyone to scatter and search for any clue. After three hours:

It was almost midnight. They were exhausted. Ted thought of taking the day off and search the next day. Badru leaned on a pillar, panting and completely exhausted. Just as he drank some Gatorade, he found something amiss about the pillar which he leaned on. Generally pillars were completely immovable and felt like, well, rocks. But this one seemed to feel a bit different. This felt like it had mechanical structure inside. The pillar seemed to rotate lightly. There seemed to be a metal ball bearing structure. "We should get some fine oil," noted Ted. Badru talked to the head of the site and told that all tourists should move out immediately. Soon crowds of disappointed tourists were moving out of the archaeological site. Now rotating it took some time. The metal structure seems to be ancient. After some hours, the pillar finally rotated. By the time it was evening, a small staircase can be seen under the entrance of the shaft. The discussed whether they should enter it. But the decision was already decided from the second they took this expedition. Bahiti decided to stay back. Ted and Badru ventured into it. Something was felt by Ted's foot, and suddenly the entrance of the shaft closed, sealing them in total darkness. "What should we do?" asked Badru frantically. "Let's move on," said Ted, for what else could they do.

The staircase was dark and gloomy. It went deep and deep into the darkness with no end to be seen. Ted's mind was worrying about what they were going to face in endless peril. Badru managed to flash a torchlight. They had the problem of snakes in the dark. Their walk was careful as there were cracks and breaks in their thin path. At one point, it became too narrow that they had to edge sideways. Then the path broadened again. Suffocation was also a major problem at such depths. At one point, Badru stopped and asked whether they should go any deeper. But they both knew their only chance of freedom lay in the hope that there is a way out on the other side.

After an hour or two, they noticed a shape in the distance. Soon they found out it was a door. Old words were inscribed on it. "What should we do?" asked Badru. Ted was trying to read those words which were written in Greek. Finally, after some minutes, he succeeded. "I got it," said Ted and began to read-

"Enter the trial of the fallen Lords to achieve what you seek; the twins' path may save you."

"'What is this trial of Lords?" Badru asked. "Not sure," said Ted, but he had an instinct that they would find out soon. Together they pushed the door open. There was a large room on the other side of the doorway. This was like the size of 10 main halls of palaces. It was so big that on each side stood huge statues of Kings with crowns. Ted was completely awed by how magnificent the room was. In the center, there was a rectangular vertical slab with inscriptions. Directly opposite to them, there was another gate. This was, unlike the first one, locked. The slab's inscriptions too were written in Greek. It took Ted 15 minutes to translate it. Finally, he said, "Done, here, let me tell you:

"Find the key inside a lord, but choose carefully or become prey."

"So the Key is inside one of these statues," said Badru. He kept his hands on one of it and was alarmed to see that it was hollow. "Maybe we should break it," suggested Ted. "Good idea," said Badru, and he took a big rock and threw it at the statue. Suddenly, Badru yelped. Dozens of snakes emerged from the statue and leaped forward with a cunning hiss. Badru jerked back and ran. Ted was staring at the snakes in horror. Ted now remembered the story of the Mayan twins, and suddenly it struck him. The snakes drew nearer and nearer. Badru was hyperventilating and sweating profusely. Ted told Badru, "Remember the story of the Mayan twins; they used a mosquito to find the real Lords of Death." The snakes hissed and moved rapidly toward them. The snakes were vicious and scaly. Ted was frightened and felt his heart pounding on his chest. Badru and Ted desperately searched for a clue on the statue. Fortunately, the statue right next to them had a symbol of a mosquito. Ted broke it with a rock and found a bronze key as the huge statues collapsed into shards. The snakes leaped forward just as Ted opened the gate and sprinted out of the room while closing the gate. Now both were breathing heavily. "You are the worst companion," said Ted. Badru just glared. Then the two seemed to realize the room they were in. This room was comparatively smaller and had no statues. It just had two benches made of rock and a rectangular slab with inscriptions just like the last one. And a gate on the opposite side was locked. As Badru inspected the chairs, he found that both chairs had a glass bowl with a bad-smelling liquid. Badru guessed one must be filled with acid. Also, both chairs had a writing in Greek. Ted quickly translated the slab and said it says:

"Do not fall for the tricks of the Lords, the key is in one of the chairs."

"So, why don't you translate the words on the chairs too?" asked Badru. Ted proceeded to do that and found out that one chair says 'Hun Hunahpu' while the other says 'Hunahpu'. Ted thought for a moment. Badru was scrutinizing Ted's face when he finally laughed and placed his hand inside the bowl of the chair which says 'Hunahpu' and found a key. Badru was astounded. "How did you know? If there was a mistake, your hand would have burned," asked Badru incuriously. Ted smiled and said, "In the story, the first pair of twins were the ones who fell for the trick while the second pair escaped, Here Hun Hunahpu must be referring to the one Hunahpu who was the father of Hunahpu." "Our expedition seems to be closely tied to the story of the Mayan twins," he concluded. "So what was the next challenge they faced?" asked Badru. Ted frowned, "Hmm, I am not so sure, I think it has something to do with balls and heads." "Well, let's go," Badru sprinted toward the door. Ted followed suit and opened the gate.

The sight that greeted them was a complete shock. There was a long rectangular pond in the long narrow room. At the center of it, there was a scepter similar to the one Ted found in Atlantis. It was brighter than anything made by humans. The room had five arches. The first two were made of rocks and the first had symbol of laurel while second had symbol of feather. The third one was made of bronze. The fourth one was also made of stone, but unlike the first two, it was plain. The first one was the one which grabbed their attention, it seemed to be made of iron, except the iron was pitch black with silver letters engraved on it in an unknown language to Ted On the far end of the narrow stretch, there was an exit from which light was possibly coming. The dark waters seemed pitch black. Ted and Badru stared at it open-mouthed. Badru thought he saw a movement in the waters, but it was hard to tell since the water was dark. Badru whispered, "I think there is something in the water." Ted went pale. Thoughts of the creature he encountered underwater rushed into his mind. He had researched and found out it was a machimosauras rex. The creature was supposed to be extinct thousands of years ago but seemed to have somehow survived and caused the destruction of Atlantis. Ted brushed aside these thoughts and looked at the dark waters. "Should we swim?" asked Badru. "No, we should edge around the side of the room," decided Ted. So they edged around the side of the room. The water rippled. Ted signaled for Badru to stop. The rippling increased and abruptly stopped. "Go," whispered Ted. Badru did so and approached the scepter, stretching his arms to reach it. The water rippled again. Badru pulled back his arm. After a few seconds, he stretched his arms again, reached the scepter, and pulled it. It came out softly and cleanly. Then all hell broke loose. The room started shaking wildly. Ted nearly stumbled into the waters. Badru pulled him and shouted, "We should go now!" They both ran toward the exit. Cracks began to appear on the upper section. Dust and rocks fell down. They both ran toward the opening. Sunlight began to appear as they hurried. Amidst everything, a deafening mighty roar could be heard. Badru froze in his tracks. The sound was louder than any living being's sound. Ted pulled him and they went out of the opening. They leaped into the light just as the rocks fell and the cavern was sealed for all eternity.

"The best view comes after the hardest climb."

– Unknown

CHAPTER 18

Ted and Badru were panting from the shock. The scepter lay at their feet. They had come out on the side of a mountain with extraordinary scenery. A golden Barley field lay ahead of them. Birds chirped and insects buzzed around. It had a serene landscape with rolling green hills and bright blue sky. The wind was perfect and relieving. The woods stood above them on the mountain's top. The sun wasn't too hot. A rejuvenating pristine lake could be seen with white swans. This exquisite moment calmed their souls. "What the hell was that thing?" asked Badru. "I would rather not want to find out," replied Ted. Ted took a moment to relax and thought of the inscription which started his expedition. He thought he should go through it once again, and so he did.

"To defeat Chronos, the monster, hunt the weapon of gods which holds the power to unite the heavens and hell. Find it in the land which lost its right on land and was swallowed by an ocean of despair, but remember what sunk the kingdom was not only a monster, but a

being equal to a hundred monsters. So terrifying the true demon is, that the name of it is untold and its true boundaries' bonds are the shackles which chain it to water, unable to set foot on land. Find Hunahpu and conquer DEIMOS.

Now the second lies with the oracle of Apollo, the Cancer shows it. Remember the hero's oath, find the three, older than rocks. Find Xbalanque and conquer Phobos. And then you may conquer war itself."

He already knew the meaning of the first part. It was in order to defeat the creature, we needed antimatter. It had enough power to converge the entire world into one or destroy it into many. They found the first one, or Hunahpu, in Atlantis, which was the kingdom that sunk into the ocean. The machimosauras too apparently played a part in its destruction. The machimosauras is unable to come onto land.

Hmm Deimos, he is the God of Terror. The machimosaurus radiated pure terror.

Now the second part - It says that the Xbalanque or the second antimatter lies in The Oracle of Delphi. But Ted was confused about the lines saying hero's oath and the three. Perhaps it was a mark to find out the pillar which they rotated. So did he miss any mark which always hinted that the pillar should be rotated? Then he remembered Delphi is a ruin so the mark had probably been destroyed under the sands of time. Then it says conquer Phobos, who was the God of Fear. There is a layer of difference between terror and fear. Terror is public and feared by everyone while fear is a personal thing which can get under your skin. The machimosauras radiated terror, while the snakes and the acid bowl radiated fear. Since we conquered both fear and terror which is Phobos and Deimos, it might mean we conquered war itself or their father Ares, the God of War.

"What should we do now?" asked Badru.

Ted smiled at his friend and quoted,

"The future is uncertain... but this uncertainty is at the very heart of human creativity."

– Ilya Prigogine

Epilogue

2457 CE. The war is finally over. The world is blackened and burnt. Nuclear radiation has increased across the world. Plants cannot grow on this toxic soil. The water level has been reduced to 36 percent of the water level of 2450 CE. This apocalyptic scenario was the price of industrial civilization. Buildings were pounded to the ground. The human population rose immensely. Space colonization has been established. Humans were boarding to leave their home. Antimatter's discovery now powered all their machines. Terraformers were sent to the next solar system a hundred years ago to make it habitable for human civilization. But the thing which shocked them was the fact that the Bermuda Triangle was found to be a traversable wormhole. Traversable wormholes would allow travel in both directions from one part of the universe to another part of that same universe very quickly or would allow travel from one universe to another. The possibility of traversable wormholes in general relativity was first demonstrated in a 1973 paper by Homer Ellis and independently in a 1973 paper by K. A. Bronnikov. The most interesting thing is the fact that they could be used for time travel if used properly. Time travel came into reality. Humans could change their future by modifying their past. Special vehicles were built for this purpose. Completely autonomous machines were built for sustaining the effects of time travel. They had Nanotech capable of materializing objects and can even generate a huge blast destroying anything in its path.

These machines were named the Chronos Series, named after the Titan of Time.

TRAVERSABLE WORMHOLES:

"The distinction between the past, present, and future is only a stubbornly persistent illusion."

Albert Einstein